Pam's Secret

by Margaret Adams

Pam's Secret
Text copyright © Margaret Adams 2008
Illustrations copyright © Ian Bobb 2008
Edited by Catherine White

First published and distributed in 2008 by Gatehouse Media Limited

Printed by Wallace Printers, Westhoughton

ISBN: 978-1-84231-050-2

British Library Cataloguing-in-Publication Data:
A catalogue record for this book is available from the British Library

Gatehouse Media Limited provides an opportunity for writers to express their thoughts and feelings on aspects of their lives. The views expressed are not necessarily those of the publishers.

Author's Thanks

I should like to thank my colleague, Anne Mitchell, a good friend and proofreader; Amanda for reading *Pam's Secret* first; my husband, Roy, for cooking the dinner when I'm writing; and Maggie Harnew at www.skillsworkshop.org for her encouragement.

Chapter 1 - The secret

Pam worked in the supermarket.

The supermarket was called Asco.

She had worked at the supermarket

for a long time.

She liked her job.

Every morning,

Pam put the bread out.

This was so the customers would see it

and find what they wanted to buy.

Pam liked the smell of the bread.

Pam had a secret.

She was in love with her boss.

She had not told anyone.

None of the people at work

knew her secret.

None of her family knew her secret.

The boss did not know her secret.

She did not want anyone to know.

It was her secret.

Chapter 2 - Jenny

One day,

Pam was putting out the bread.

She could see her boss.

He was very good looking.

Pam liked to look at him.

He came to where

Pam was putting out the bread.

There was a young woman with him.

She was very good looking too.

"Pam, this is Jenny.

She has come to work here too.

I would like you to look after her today

please," said her boss.

Pam was pleased to show Jenny
what to do.

Pam was very pleased to do
what her boss asked her.

Chapter 3 - Friends

Every day,
Pam and Jenny worked together.
Jenny was funny.
She made Pam laugh
and soon they were good friends.
This was nice for Pam
because she did not have many friends.
It was nice for Jenny too
because she did not know the other
people at work.

One day, Jenny saw
that Pam was looking at the boss.
Pam was looking at him a lot!
"He is very good looking," said Jenny.
"Do you like him?"

Pam was very surprised.

She had never told anyone her secret.

She thought she would trust Jenny

because they were friends.

"I love him," Pam said,
"but please do not tell anyone
because it is a secret."

"You can trust me," said Jenny.

Chapter 4 - The end of being friends

The next morning

Pam came to work at Asco,

the same as she did every morning.

But today was not the same.

People kept looking at her.

Some people were laughing at her.

Why?

Pam went to hang up her coat.

Dan was there.

Dan was a nice man.

He worked at Asco too.

His job was to stack the shelves.

He put the tins on the shelves.

Pam liked him.

He was nice and kind.

"Why are people laughing at me, Dan?"
Pam said.

"They are laughing
because Jenny has told them
you love the boss," said Dan.

"But that was a secret," said Pam.

She was very upset.

When Pam saw Jenny,

she did not talk to her again.

Chapter 5 - The office

Two weeks later,

Pam still did not talk to Jenny.

She had thought they were friends

but Jenny was not a good friend.

She had told other people her secret.

It was sad because

Pam had liked having a friend.

Pam had put all the bread out today.

It was a nice day

and Pam was feeling a bit better now.

People had stopped laughing at her.

Now she had to go to the office.

She had to take in some forms from

the man who had delivered the bread.

She liked him. He was nice.

When she got to the office,
she knocked on the door.
There was no answer
so she opened the door.
She was going to put the forms
on the desk.

But when she opened the door,
the boss was in there.
So was Jenny.
They were kissing.

Pam was very upset
and she ran out of the office.
She was crying.

Chapter 6 - The boss's secret

It was a few weeks later now.

Everybody knew

about the boss and Jenny.

Jenny was not the nice person

that Pam had thought she was.

She knew Pam had been

in love with the boss,

but she did not care.

She wanted him.

The boss gave Jenny the best jobs to do.

People who worked in the shop

were not pleased

because it was not fair.

One day,
a woman came into the shop
and asked to see the boss.
She had a little girl
and a little boy with her.

Pam took her up to his office.
Jenny was standing close by
when she knocked at the door.

The boss let her in.
He was surprised to see the woman.
He was surprised to see the little girl.
He was surprised to see the little boy.

He was surprised to see Jenny too.

"Daddy!" said the children.

"Darling," said the woman,

"what time will you be home for dinner?"

The boss had not told anyone
he was married.
He had a secret too.

THE END

A comprehensive set of tutor resources, mapped to the Adult Literacy Core Curriculum, is available to support this book:

Pam's Secret Tutor Resources CD-Rom
ISBN: 978-1-84231-055-7

Coming soon in the Supermarket Stories series:

Bob's Problem
ISBN: 978-1-84231-056-4

Bob's Problem Tutor Resources CD-Rom
ISBN: 978-1-84231-057-1

Author's Note

I have written short stories for individual students on quite a few different occasions, usually to help them practise a particular letter pattern, consonant blend, digraph etc., or to meet an observed need of the particular student.

Pam's Secret is the first of the *Supermarket Stories*. It was initially written for an individual student who comes to Essential English, a literacy class within the ACRES consortium in East Sussex.

The main intention of the series is to give Entry Level students a story to read. I have often found that books for students at this level don't always have a story as such, and, as someone who enjoys stories, I wanted to give my students the same opportunity. I wanted to show that reading can be a pleasure, not just a necessity.

They are adult stories with adult themes. I have written them so that students can read a chapter per session and I have finished each chapter at a point that will encourage the reader to come back for more.

Each chapter can be used to practise specific learning aims, although this does not have to be the case. The supporting resources also check comprehension and encourage the reader to think more broadly about the text. I hope that this will encourage the reader to see the relevance of reading stories - *they make you think, not just read.*

Margaret Adams

Gatehouse Books®

Gatehouse Books are written for older teenagers and adults who are developing their basic reading and writing or English language skills.

The format of our books is clear and uncluttered. The language is familiar and the text is often line-broken, so that each line ends at a natural pause.

Gatehouse Books are widely used within Adult Basic Education throughout the English speaking world. They are also a valuable resource within the Prison Education Service and Probation Services, Social Services and secondary schools - both in basic skills and ESOL teaching situations.

Catalogue available

Gatehouse Media Limited
PO Box 965
Warrington
WA4 9DE

Tel/Fax: 01925 267778
E-mail: info@gatehousebooks.com
Website: www.gatehousebooks.com